THE GRAPHIC
SHAKESPEARE SERIES

THE TEMPEST

Published by
Evans Brothers Limited
2A Portman Mansions
Chiltern Street
London W1U 6NR

Reprinted 2006 (twice), 2007

Designed by Design Systems Ltd.

British Library Cataloguing in Publication Data
Burningham, Hilary
  The tempest
  Student's book. – (Shakespeare plays)
  1. Shakespeare, William, 1564-1616. Tempest – Juvenile literature
  I. Title
  822.3'3

ISBN 0 237 519100
13-digit ISBN (from 1 Jan 2007) 978 0 237 51910 0

Printed in Malta by Gutenberg Press.

THE GRAPHIC SHAKESPEARE SERIES

THE TEMPEST

RETOLD BY HILARY BURNINGHAM
ILLUSTRATED BY CHARITY LINCOLN

EVANS BROTHERS LIMITED

THE CHARACTERS IN THE PLAY

Prospero — a magician, formerly Duke of Milan

Miranda — Prospero's daughter

Alonso — King of Naples

Ferdinand — son of the King of Naples

Sebastian — brother of the King of Naples

Antonio — Prospero's brother; he became Duke of Milan

Gonzalo — an honest old councillor

Caliban — Prospero's slave

Ariel — an airy spirit, also Prospero's slave

Trinculo — a jester

Stephano — butler to the King of Naples

Boatswain — an officer on the ship

Juno — one of the gods in Prospero's play

Adrian — a lord from Naples

Francisco — another lord from Naples

PORTRAIT GALLERY

Prospero

Miranda

Alonso

Ferdinand

Sebastian

Antonio

Gonzalo

Caliban

Ariel

Trinculo

Stephano

Boatswain

Juno

Adrian

ACT 1

A ship was caught in a terrible storm at sea. The Captain, the Boatswain and the sailors were doing everything they could to save the ship.

Some very important people were on the ship: the King of Naples, his son the Prince, and many nobles. They were all very frightened. They were shouting and arguing with each other, and with the boatswain[1] and his sailors.

Suddenly, the sailors shouted that the ship was sinking. The sailors and the passengers were all sure that they were going to die. They would drown in the sea.

---

[1]boatswain – officer in charge of the sails and the ropes, pronounced "bo'sun"

BOATSWAIN: Yet again? What do you here? Shall we give
            o'er and drown? Have you a mind to sink?
SEBASTIAN: A pox o' your throat, you bawling,
            blasphemous, incharitable dog!
BOATSWAIN: Work you, then.
ANTONIO: Hang, cur, hang, you whoreson, insolent
            noisemaker! We are less afraid to be
            drowned than thou art.

Prospero and his daughter Miranda lived on an island nearby. Prospero could do magic.

Miranda had seen the ship in the storm. She had heard the people on the ship crying and shouting for help. Miranda felt very sorry for everyone on the ship.

She asked her father if he had caused the storm.

Prospero told her not to worry. No one had been harmed or hurt. The storm was part of a plan.

MIRANDA: O, I have suffered
With those that I saw suffer! A brave vessel,
Who had, no doubt, some noble creature in her,
Dashed all to pieces. O, the cry did knock
Against my very heart!

Prospero took off his magic cloak. It was time to tell Miranda about the island. It was time to tell her why they lived there.

His story started twelve years before when he, Prospero, was the Duke of Milan. Miranda was his daughter. Prospero loved to read. He spent all his time in his library. Antonio, his brother, began to take over in his place. He became more and more powerful.

Antonio made a plan with the King of Naples. Antonio would pay the king a lot of money. He would then get rid of Prospero. The King of Naples would make sure that Antonio became Duke of Milan in place of Prospero.

Miranda was so shocked that she started to cry. Antonio was Prospero's brother, yet he plotted to take his place. Antonio must be a very evil man.

PROSPERO: I, thus neglecting worldy ends, all dedicated
To closeness and the bettering of my mind
With that which, but by being so retired,
O'er-prized all popular rate, in my false brother
Awaked an evil nature.

Antonio was afraid to kill Prospero. All the people still loved him. Instead, he and Miranda, who was only a baby, were put on a leaky old boat. They were sent out to sea.

A kind friend called Gonzalo helped Prospero and his daughter. He gave them clothes and other things they would need. Best of all, he got some of Prospero's books for him. Prospero could keep on studying and learning.

So they came to their island, father and daughter. For Prospero, Miranda was a reason to live. He taught her many things. He was a very good teacher.

Now, his enemies had come to the island. This was his chance to get even with them.

MIRANDA: Alack, what trouble
          Was I then to you!
PROSPERO: O, a cherubim
          Thou wast that did preserve me.

Prospero's plan began. He called his helper – a spirit named Ariel. Ariel could fly, swim, and ride on clouds. He could make himself visible or invisible.

In the middle of the storm, Ariel visited the ship. There had been huge waves, flashes of lightening, fire and noise. Everyone was terrified. It was all Prospero's magic.

Now, all the people on the ship were safely on the island. No one had drowned. The King's son, Ferdinand, was separate from the others. The sailors were asleep on the ship. The ship was safe too.

Prospero was pleased. Now he and Ariel had more work to do.

ARIEL: The King's son have I landed by himself,
Whom I left cooling of the air with sighs
In an odd angle of the isle, and sitting,
His arms in this sad knot.

Ariel wasn't sure about doing more work. He had worked hard, and Prospero had promised to set him free.

When Prospero came to the island, Ariel was trapped in a pine tree. He had been left there by an evil witch called Sycorax. Prospero had got him out of the pine tree, and he had worked for Prospero ever since. A few more tasks, and Prospero would set him free forever.

The witch, Sycorax, had a son called Caliban. He was born on the island. When Prospero first went to the island, he treated Caliban kindly. They were friends. He and Miranda taught Caliban to speak.

Caliban tried to hurt Miranda. After that, Prospero treated him roughly and made him do all the hard work.

PROSPERO: If thou neglect'st, or dost unwillingly
What I command, I'll rack thee with old cramps,
Fill all thy bones with aches, make thee roar,
That beasts shall tremble at thy din.

Ferdinand, son of the King of Naples, thought his father was dead. He was alone in another part of the island and weeping for his father.

Ariel played music and sang to him. Ferdinand followed the sound to Prospero's cave.

Miranda and Ferdinand met. Miranda had seen only two other men before: her father and Caliban. She thought that Ferdinand was both handsome and good. Ferdinand loved Miranda from the moment he saw her. He wanted to marry her. He wanted her to be his queen.

Prospero was pleased. This was all part of his plan. Suddenly, he was worried. Were things happening too quickly?

MIRANDA: There's nothing ill can dwell in such a
temple.
If the ill spirit have so fair a house,
Good things will strive to dwell with't.

Prospero decided to test Ferdinand. He wanted to be sure that Ferdinand really loved Miranda.

He spoke rudely to Ferdinand. He said that he would chain him up and give him horrible things to eat and drink. Ferdinand drew his sword, but found he could not move. That was Prospero's magic.

Ferdinand said that he felt as if he were in a prison. He didn't care. He would be happy if only he could see Miranda once a day.

Miranda was surprised at Prospero's rudeness. She didn't know that he was trying to make sure that Ferdinand really loved her.

PROSPERO: Put thy sword up, traitor,
Who mak'st a show, but dar'st not strike, thy conscience
Is so possessed with guilt. Come from thy ward!
For I can here disarm thee with this stick,
And make thy weapon drop.

ACT 2

In another part of the island, Alonso, the King of Naples, was very unhappy. He was sure that his son Ferdinand had drowned in the shipwreck. He didn't know that Ferdinand was safe and well.

Two of the men with the king were very rude to everyone else. One of these men was Sebastian, Alonso's brother. The other was Antonio. Antonio was Prospero's wicked brother. He was the brother who had sent Prospero and Miranda away. He had taken Prospero's place as the Duke of Milan.

A wise old man, Gonzalo, was trying to be cheerful. He said that they should all be happy that they were safe. Very few people escaped from shipwrecks.

Gonzalo was the kind person who had helped Prospero and Miranda many years before, when Antonio sent them away. Now he, too, was on Prospero's island.

King Alonso was too unhappy to be comforted. He was thinking about his son.

GONZALO: But for the miracle,
I mean our preservation, few in millions
Can speak like us. Then wisely, good sir, weigh
Our sorrow with our comfort.
ALONSO: Prithee, peace.

Antonio and Sebastian made fun of Gonzalo, and of Adrian, another man who tried to be cheerful.

Adrian and Gonzalo saw the island as green and pleasant, with sweet fresh air.

Sebastian and Antonio saw only dirt, sand, and rocks. To them it smelled rotten, like a swamp.

Gonzalo thought their clothes looked as fresh as when they were new. They didn't look as if they had been pulled from the sea.

Sebastian and Antonio said that Gonzalo was talking rubbish.

Another noble, Francisco, said that he was sure Alonso's son, Ferdinand, was alive. He had seen Ferdinand swimming to the shore.

Cruelly, Sebastian said that Ferdinand was gone forever.

GONZALO: My lord Sebastian,
          The truth you speak doth lack some gentleness,
          And time to speak it in. You rub the sore,
          When you should bring the plaster.

Gonzalo spoke about the island. If he were king of the island, he would make it a perfect place – no rich people, no poor people, and no fighting. Everyone would live together in peace.

Gonzalo had worked for kings and princes all his life. He knew how difficult it was to be a good leader.

Sebastian and Antonio cheered as if he really were a king. Gonzalo didn't know that they were making fun of him.

GONZALO: I would with such perfection govern, sir,
T'excel the Golden Age.
SEBASTIAN: 'Save his majesty!
ANTONIO: Long live Gonzalo!

Suddenly, Alonso, Gonzalo, Adrian and Francisco felt very sleepy. Ariel was among them, playing soft music. His magic was making them sleepy.

Gonzalo, Adrian and Francisco fell asleep straight away. King Alonso tried to stay awake. He, too, felt very tired. Sebastian and Antonio told him to go to sleep. They would make sure he was safe. The king slept.

ANTONIO: We two, my lord,
Will guard your person while you take your rest,
And watch your safety.
ALONSO: Thank you. Wondrous heavy.

Sebastian and Antonio were puzzled. Everyone else had gone to sleep. They didn't know it was Prospero's magic.

They had a chance to talk together. Antonio told Sebastian that he could imagine him wearing a crown. Sebastian was surprised. His brother Alonso was king. Alonso had two children. What chance had he to be king and to wear a crown?

Antonio said that things had changed now. Ferdinand was drowned. His sister lived far away. If they killed the sleeping Alonso, Sebastian could be king.

They drew their swords. Antonio would kill Alonso. Sebastian would kill Gonzalo. All the others would do as they were told.

Just in time, Ariel came back.

SEBASTIAN: Thy case, dear friend,
Shall be my precedent. As thou got'st Milan,
I'll come by Naples. Draw thy sword. One stroke
Shall free thee from the tribute which thou payest,
And I the King shall love thee.

Ariel sang his song loudly in Gonzalo's ear. Gonzalo awoke and shouted to wake the king and the others.

They were all surprised to see Antonio and Sebastian holding their swords. Antonio and Sebastian quickly made up an excuse. They had heard noises of wild animals. They were protecting the king.

Alonso no longer wanted to sleep. If there were wild animals on the island, he must hurry to look for his son.

SEBASTIAN: Whiles we stood here securing your repose,
Even now, we heard a hollow burst of bellowing
Like bulls, or rather lions. Did't not wake you?
It struck mine ear most terribly.

Prospero had sent Caliban to collect wood. Caliban was complaining to himself about Prospero's terrible punishments. Sometimes he was bitten, or prickly hedgehogs were put under his bare feet. Sometimes snakes bit him and hissed at him. He hated Prospero.

CALIBAN: All the infections that the sun sucks up
           From bogs, fens, flats, on Prosper fall, and make him
           By inch-meal a disease! His spirits hear me,
           And yet I needs must curse.

Caliban saw Trinculo coming. Trinculo was Alonso's jester. His job was to make the king and the nobles laugh.

Caliban thought Trinculo was sent by Prospero. He thought Trinculo would be cruel to him. He was afraid. He hid under an old cloak.

The storm was coming again. Trinculo saw Caliban and his cloak on the ground. He decided to hide under the cloak to shelter from the storm.

TRINCULO: Alas, the storm is come again. My best way is to creep under his gaberdine. There is no other shelter hereabout. Misery acquaints a man with strange bedfellows. I will here shroud till the dregs of the storm be past.

Stephano, the king's butler, was having a good time on the island. He had some wine from the ship and was getting drunk. He was singing an old sea song.

He saw Trinculo's legs and Caliban's legs sticking out from under the cloak. This must be a monster of the island. He would take the monster back to Naples. He would make a lot of money showing the monster to other people.

Caliban stuck his head out of the cloak to look at Stephano. Stephano gave him some wine.

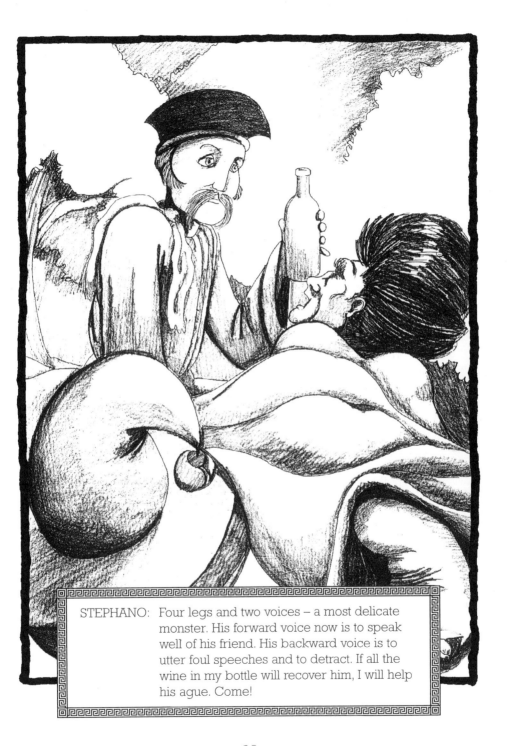

STEPHANO: Four legs and two voices – a most delicate monster. His forward voice now is to speak well of his friend. His backward voice is to utter foul speeches and to detract. If all the wine in my bottle will recover him, I will help his ague. Come!

Trinculo and Stephano were very happy to see each other. They had both escaped the shipwreck. Trinculo had swum to the shore. Stephano had floated on a wine barrel. He had saved lots of wine from the shipwreck.

Caliban had never tasted wine before. He thought wine was wonderful. He thought Stephano was wonderful. He wanted Stephano to be his new master. He wouldn't work for Prospero. He would show Stephano all the treasures of the island. Caliban's treasures were small apples, nuts, birds' eggs, and small animals to catch and eat.

They followed Ariel's music. Caliban led the way, happily singing about his new master.

CALIBAN: Ban, Ban, Cacaliban
Has a new master – get a new man!
Freedom, high-day! High-day, freedom!
Freedom, high-day, freedom!
STEPHANO: O brave monster! Lead the way.

ACT 3

Prospero was still testing Ferdinand. He wanted to be sure that Ferdinand truly loved Miranda. He made Ferdinand carry logs as Caliban did. Ferdinand was getting very tired. He kept working because he loved Miranda. He wanted to please her father.

Miranda hated to see Ferdinand getting so tired. She offered to carry some logs for him.

Ferdinand had liked some women before he met Miranda. He had never known a woman who seemed to be so perfect. He thought his father Alonso was dead. That would mean that he was King of Naples. Even if he were king, he would carry logs for Prospero, because he loved Miranda.

Miranda was so happy that she cried.

FERDINAND: I,
Beyond all limit of what else i'th'world,
Do love, prize, honour you.
MIRANDA: I am a fool
To weep at what I am glad of.

Miranda and Ferdinand were in love and wanted to be married.

Prospero was happy about Miranda and Ferdinand, but he had some other things to do. He wanted to be Duke of Milan again. He had to make sure that Ferdinand and Miranda would be happy together. He went to study his Book of Magic. He would be doing more magic before the day was over.

PROSPERO: I'll to my book,
For yet ere suppertime must I perform
Much business appertaining.

Stephano, Trinculo and Caliban were getting more and more drunk.

Ariel imitated Trinculo's voice, making them quarrel among themselves.

CALIBAN: As I told thee before, I am subject to a tyrant, a
sorcerer, that by his cunning cheated me of the
island.
ARIEL: Thou liest.
CALIBAN (*to Trinculo*): Thou liest, thou jesting monkey, thou.
I would my valiant master would destroy thee!
I do not lie.

Caliban wanted Stephano to be his master. He wanted Stephano to murder Prospero and become king of the island. Perhaps Stephano would marry Miranda. He told Stephano when Prospero would be asleep.

Ariel heard the whole plan. He would warn Prospero.

He played his pipe. He was invisible, but Stephano and the others could hear the music. They followed the sound of the music.

STEPHANO: This will prove a brave kingdom to me,
where I shall have my music for nothing.
CALIBAN: When Prospero is destroyed.
STEPHANO: That shall be by and by.

Alonso, Gonzalo, and the others, were still searching for Ferdinand. The two old men were getting very tired. Sebastian and Antonio planned to kill Alonso at the next opportunity.

Suddenly, they heard music. Some strange creatures carried in food. They put the food on a table and disappeared. Prospero was working his magic again.

ALONSO: What harmony is this? My good friends, hark!
GONZALO: Marvellous sweet music!

The king, Gonzalo, and the others, were hungry. They wanted to eat the food. Just as they were going to begin, the food disappeared. Ariel appeared on the table.

The men drew their swords.

Ariel told them they would not be able to lift their swords. Ariel reminded Alonso, Antonio and Sebastian of what they had done to Prospero and Miranda.

Now, Alonso had lost his son. They had done evil deeds. None of them would have any peace.

ARIEL: But remember –
For that's my business to you – that you three
From Milan did supplant good Prosper,
Exposed unto the sea, which hath requit it,
Him and his innocent child; for which foul deed
The powers, delaying, not forgetting, have
Incensed the seas and shores, yea, all the creatures
Against your peace.

Ariel spoke to Alonso about Prospero and Miranda. Alonso thought his crime had caused his son's death. He wanted to drown himself as well. He rushed to the sea. Sebastian and Antonio followed him.

Gonzalo sent the younger men after them. Alonso, Sebastian and Antonio might do something foolish. After all these years, they were feeling ashamed of what they had done to Prospero.

GONZALO: All three of them are desperate. Their great guilt,
Like poison given to work a great time after,
Now 'gins to bit the spirits.

ACT 4

Ferdinand passed all Prospero's tests. He and Miranda could be married.

Until they were married, they could talk and get to know each other. Miranda and Ferdinand were happy.

PROSPERO: Sit then and talk with her; she is thine own.

Prospero put on a special show for Miranda and Ferdinand. Gods blessed their marriage. There was music, and singing.

The show ended with a dance.

JUNO: Honour, riches, marriage blessing,
        Long continuance, and increasing,
        Hourly joys be still upon you!
        Juno sings her blessings on you.

Suddenly, Prospero caused all the show to vanish. He remembered that Caliban, Stephano and Trinculo were trying to kill him.

Ferdinand and Miranda were very puzzled. The show had ended and Prospero seemed upset.

Prospero told them that the actors in the play were all spirits. When their play was finished, they disappeared. They weren't real. Nothing was real.

He called Ariel and told him to fetch Caliban, Trinculo and Sebastian. Prospero was going to punish them, especially Caliban.

PROSPERO: Be cheerful, sir.
Our revels now are attended. These our actors,
As I foretold you, were all spirits, and
Are melted into air, into thin air.

Ariel led Caliban, Stephano and Trinculo into a pool of water. They were all wet and smelled horrible. Next, he led them to Prospero's cave.

Outside the cave, Ariel hung beautiful glittering clothes.

Trinculo and Stephano started fighting over the clothes. They wasted time. Caliban wanted them to kill Prospero while they had the chance. He thought they were stupid to be quarrelling about clothes. Prospero might catch them all and there would be a terrible punishment.

Prospero and Ariel came with spirits in the shape of horrible dogs and hounds. Caliban, Trinculo and Stephano ran away with the dogs after them.

PROSPERO: Fury, Fury! There, Tyrant, there! Hark, hark!
Go, charge my goblins that they grind their
joints
With dry convulsions, shorten up their sinews
With aged cramps, and more pinch-spotted
make them
Than pard or cat o'mountain.

ARIEL: Hark, they roar!

ACT 5

Prospero's plan was coming to its end. Now, it was time to deal with Alonso, Antonio and Sebastian. Prospero sent Ariel to fetch them. He wanted them to feel sorry for treating him and Miranda so badly. When his plan was finished, he would give up his magic.

Ariel brought them back. They stood in Prospero's magic circle. Prospero had them under a spell. They had to listen while he spoke to them. He reminded them of all the bad things they had done. At last, he forgave them.

None of them knew who he was or recognised him. Ariel brought the clothes he used to wear as Duke of Milan, and helped him put them on.

Very soon, Ariel would be free. He sang a happy song about how he would live when he had his freedom. Prospero sent him to fetch the Captain of the king's ship, the boatswain, and the sailors. They had been asleep all this time.

PROSPERO: Not one of them
That yet looks on me, or would know me. Ariel,
Fetch me the hat and rapier in my cell.
I will discase me, and myself present
As I was sometime Milan. Quickly, spirit!
Thou shalt ere long be free.

Prospero woke Alonso and the others from their trance[1]. He told them he was the Duke of Milan, sent away years before. Alonso asked to be forgiven.

Prospero quietly warned Sebastian and Antonio that he knew what they had planned. He could get them into serious trouble. Antonio must give him back his title as Duke of Milan.

Next, he had a wonderful surprise for Alonso: he showed him Miranda and Ferdinand happily playing chess together. Alonso could not believe his eyes.

Miranda met her future father-in-law, Alonso, King of Naples, and his nobles. Miranda thought they were all very beautiful.

[1]trance – a kind of magic sleep

MIRANDA: O, wonder!
How many goodly creatures are there here!
How beauteous mankind is! O brave new world,
That has such people in't!

Ariel brought the Captain and the Boatswain from the king's ship. Their news was that the ship was ready to sail. It was in excellent condition. The sailors were ready.

Finally, Ariel brought back Caliban, Stephano and Trinculo. Stephano and Trinculo were still very drunk. Caliban was terrified of Prospero. He thought he would get a terrible punishment.

Prospero told Caliban to clean his cave. Trinculo and Stephano could help. If they did a good job, perhaps he would forgive them.

PROSPERO: Go, sirrah, to my cell.
Take with you your companions. As you look
To have my pardon, trim it handsomely.

Prospero was leaving his island. He planned to go to Naples for the wedding of Ferdinand and Miranda and then to Milan. He would be Duke of Milan again.

Ariel had one more task. He must make sure the sea was calm, with good winds to blow the ships safely home. After that, he was free. Prospero said goodbye to Ariel and goodbye to his magic.

PROSPERO: I'll deliver all,
And promise you calm seas, auspicious gales,
And sail so expeditious, that shall catch
Your royal fleet far off. – My Ariel, chick,
That is in thy charge. Then to the elements
Be free, and fare thou well.